Teddy Roosevelt
and the Treasure of Ursa Major

Teddy Roosevelt
and the Treasure of Ursa Major

ADAPTED BY RONALD KIDD

FROM THE PLAY BY TOM ISBELL
Commissioned by the
John F. Kennedy Center for the Performing Arts
and the White House Historical Association

ILLUSTRATED BY ARD HOYT

SIMON & SCHUSTER BOOKS FOR YOUNG READERS
NEW YORK   LONDON   TORONTO   SYDNEY

SIMON & SCHUSTER BOOKS FOR YOUNG READERS
An imprint of Simon & Schuster Children's Publishing Division
1230 Avenue of the Americas, New York, New York 10020
This book is a work of fiction. Any references to historical events, real people, or real locales are used fictitiously. Other names, characters, places, and incidents are products of the author's imagination, and any resemblance to actual events or locales or persons, living or dead, is entirely coincidental.
Copyright © 2008 by the John F. Kennedy Center for the Performing Arts
All rights reserved, including the right of reproduction in whole or in part in any form. • Adapted by Ronald Kidd
SIMON & SCHUSTER BOOKS FOR YOUNG READERS is a trademark of Simon & Schuster, Inc. For information about special discounts for bulk purchases, please contact Simon & Schuster Special Sales at 1-866-506-1949 or business@simonandschuster.com.
The Simon & Schuster Speakers Bureau can bring authors to your live event. For more information or to book an event, contact the Simon & Schuster Speakers Bureau at 1-866-248-3049 or visit our website at www.simonspeakers.com.
Also available in an Aladdin hardcover edition
Book design by Lisa Vega • The text for this book is set in Sabon.
The illustrations for this book are rendered in pen and ink.
Manufactured in the United States of America • 0812 OFF
First Simon & Schuster Books for Young Readers paperback edition January 2011
2 4 6 8 10 9 7 5 3
The Library of Congress has cataloged the hardcover edition as follows:
Kidd, Ronald.
Teddy Roosevelt and the treasure of Ursa Major/adapted by Ronald Kidd; illustrated by Ard Hoyt.
p. cm.—(The Kennedy Center presents: Capital kids)
"From a play [by Tom Isbell] commissioned by the John F. Kennedy Center for the Performing Arts and the White House Historical Association."
Summary: President Theodore Roosevelt's children search for clues to a hidden treasure in the White House.
ISBN 978-1-4169-4857-5 (hc)
1.Roosevelt, Theodore, 1858–1919—Family—Juvenile Fiction. [1. Roosevelt, Theofore, 1858–1919—Family—Fiction. 2. White House (Washington, D.C.)—Fiction. 3. Buried treasure—Fiction. 4. Brothers and sisters—Fiction.]
I. Hoyt, Ard, ill. II.Isbell, Tom, 1957– III. Title.
PZ7.K5315Te2008 • [Fic]—dc22 • 2007025430
ISBN 978-1-4169-4860-5 (pbk) • ISBN 978-1-4424-1724-3 (eBook)
This book is based on the play of the same name, written by Tom Isbell, which was co-commissioned and co-produced by the John F. Kennedy Center for the Performing Arts and the White House Historical Asociation.
It was produced in the Kennedy Center Family Theater in the fall of 2006.

This series is dedicated to Debra Hansen with eternal gratitude for sharing a bit of your vast talent with me and for being my grandmother.

—A. H.

Contents

Foreword by Laura Bush

Teddy Roosevelt and the Treasure of Ursa Major

If your home could talk, what secrets would it tell? What would it say about the people who lived there before you, in the rooms where you now eat, sleep, and play? Would your home reveal the mysteries hidden beneath its floorboards, and within its walls? What if its most closely guarded secret was . . . buried treasure?

In *Teddy Roosevelt and the Treasure of Ursa Major*, you'll follow three adventurous children as they unravel the mysteries of *their* home. You'll decipher clues alongside Kermit, Ethel, and Archie Roosevelt—the children of President Theodore Roosevelt. And their home just happens to be one of the most famous buildings in the world—the White House!

During your search, you'll read about what it was like for Kermit, Ethel, and Archie to grow up in the Roosevelt household, with their exotic pets and their hilarious antics. You'll learn about their father, one of America's most respected conservationists, war heroes, peacemakers, and presidents. And you'll discover fascinating stories of the White House— stories that, like the beautiful home itself, belong to all Americans.

President Bush and I are inspired by the history we see around us every day in the White House, including many of the rooms, paintings, and artifacts you'll read about in this book. In fact, when the Roosevelt children find an early clue in their father's desk, they're investigating a historic piece of furniture still used by U.S. presidents—including President Bush— to this day.

Teddy Roosevelt and the Treasure of Ursa Major tells the stories of many extraordinary Americans who've called the White House home. But as you'll soon discover, presidents, first ladies, and their children are ordinary families just like yours and mine. And as the Roosevelt children learn, you don't have to live in the White House to unearth the riches of the past. In your local libraries and museums, you can learn about the history of your own home or community—and the people who lived there before you. You may be surprised by what you find. After all, as Kermit, Ethel, and Archie discover, some of life's most valuable treasures are found where you least expect them.

Of course, one of the very best places to find hidden treasures is in a good book. The Roosevelts' adventure starts with a great book called *Treasure Island*, and leads them on a thrilling chase throughout the White House, across the landscape of American history, and to the limits of their imagination. I encourage you to find many exciting adventures in your favorite books. And I hope you'll begin right here, in the pages of *Teddy Roosevelt and the Treasure of Ursa Major*.

Laura Bush

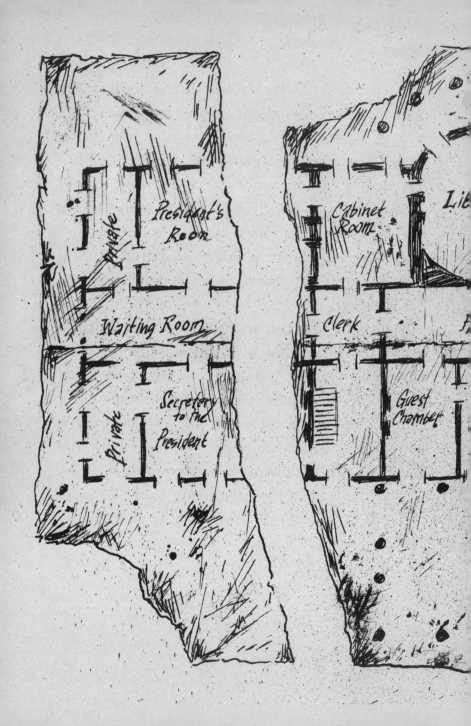

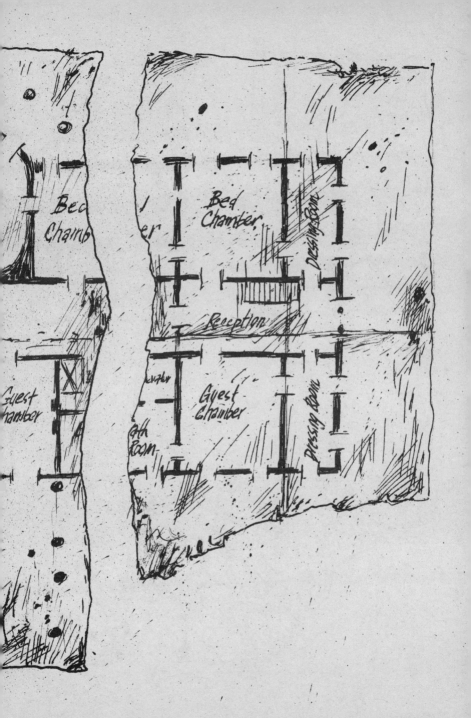

Teddy Roosevelt

and the Treasure of Ursa Major

1.

The Haunted House

"Find the treasure, Archie," said the ghost.

It appeared out of nowhere, a dim shape with gleaming eyes and a voice like sandpaper.

"B-but I'm just a kid," I said.

"Find the treasure before the others," said the ghost. "Find the treasure. Find the treasure. Find the treasure. . . ."

The voice faded out, and the shape melted away.

My name is Archie Roosevelt. I'm eleven years old. I live with my father, mother, five brothers and sisters, a rabbit, a pony, a macaw, and a ghost.

I never knew my house was haunted. But then, there were a lot of things I didn't know about it. Once, soldiers set it on fire and burned it to the ground. It has a desk made from an abandoned sailing ship. And according to legend, it's filled with secret passageways.

Oh, there's one other thing I learned about it. They say that somewhere, among the rooms or inside the walls, there's a hidden treasure.

You've probably heard of my house. You may have even been there. It's the White House. My father is Theodore Roosevelt, president of the United States.

I found out about the treasure, the ghost, and all the rest one dark, stormy night. The night started normally enough—well, normally for my family.

I came running into the library, holding a cage containing my latest pet. "Hey, Pop, look what I caught. It's a badger!"

My father was putting on his tie. Leaning down, he squinted at the cage. "That's not a badger. It's a mouth with a leg at each corner."

My fifteen-year-old brother, Kermit, clomped by on stilts. "He didn't catch that badger. We both did."

Ethel twirled around, dancing to music that only she heard. "I don't care who caught it. I think it's disgusting." Ethel was thirteen and believed she was smarter than anyone in the room. She was, if you only counted her and the badger.

My father glanced in the mirror and straightened his tie. He has a proud chin, a bristling mustache, and little glasses that he balances on his nose. Some people say he's short and stocky, but to me he's ten feet tall.

He turned to his valet, James Amos, who was standing by as usual, perfectly dressed and in control. "James, did you see Mrs. Roosevelt off to her carriage?"

"Yes, sir. Right on time."

I guess my mother needed a rest. She had all the duties of the First Lady, and in her spare time she raised six children. The two oldest, Alice and Teddy Junior, had already moved out. Earlier that day she had taken the youngest, Quentin, to visit my aunt. That left Kermit, Ethel, and me.

"Did the Russian ambassador arrive yet?" my father asked.

"Due any minute," said James.

"Pop," said Kermit, wobbling on his stilts, "are the Russians and Japanese still fighting?"

"Yes, but only until I get them in a room together. Then we'll iron this thing out."

I decided it was time to talk about important things.

"Can we get a rabbit?" I asked.

Ethel twirled past me. "You've already got a rabbit."

"That's just it," I said. "The rabbit needs a friend."

"Very well, we'll get another rabbit," said my father. "James, make a note. And I need a shave."

He went to his desk and picked up a sheaf of documents in one hand and a half dozen newspapers in the other. My father likes to do several things at once. He says it's his way of giving the American people their money's worth.

Settling into a chair, he opened one of the newspapers and began to read. As James lathered him up, a woman entered the room carrying a bag. Her gray hair was tied up in a bun, and she seemed nervous.

My father looked up from the paper. "Ah, you must be the new governess. Mrs. Gruffit, is it?"

"Duffit. Mrs. Duffit, sir."

He motioned to James. "This is my friend, James

Amos. They say I'm in charge, but he runs the place."

James nodded. "As smoothly as possible, all things considered. Welcome."

I thought Mrs. Duffit might like to meet my badger, so I picked up the cage and showed it to her. For some reason, she screamed.

"Don't worry," I said. "He bites legs and ankles, but never faces."

"There's good news," she said.

I smiled. "His name is Josiah. I think he's wonderific."

"Don't mind Archie," said Ethel. "He likes to make up new words by combining old ones."

I tried to explain. "So *wonderific* is a cross between—"

"*Wonderful* and *terrific*," said Kermit. "We get it, Archie."

"How come you don't let me finish my sentences?" I asked.

He tweaked my nose. "Because I know what you're going to say before you finish saying it."

Meanwhile, my father had moved on to other

things. "Mrs. Luffit, what do you know about national conservation?"

"Duffit," she said. "Um, not much."

"Is there any law that prevents me from turning an island into a federal bird reservation?"

"Not that I know of," she said.

"Bully!" said my father. "Then I so declare it."

James looked up from the lather. "Sir, the Senate may have other ideas."

"When don't they have other ideas? There are so many crooks in there that when they call the roll, the senators don't know whether to answer 'Present' or 'Not guilty'!"

"Good one, sir," said James.

"I thought so," said my father.

The two of them are always joking around. Sometimes it's almost like they have their own private language.

"Sir," James said, "where shall we put the Russian ambassador when he comes? The Red Room?"

"Too bright," said my father.

"The Green Room?"

"Too green."

"The Blue Room?"

My father nodded. "That's a calming color. It should put him at ease."

"Very good, sir."

"Of course," said my father, "as blind as he is, we could put him in the broom closet and he wouldn't know the difference."

I noticed Mrs. Duffit standing beside her bag, fidgeting. She said, "I've been meaning to ask. What happened to the last governess?"

My father looked up at James. "How's she doing, by the way?"

"The hospital expects to release her any day now."

Mrs. Duffit stared at them, then staggered back and sat down—right on the badger's cage! She screamed again and shot up in the air. We burst out laughing. Mrs. Duffit was turning out to be all right.

When James finished the shave, my father wiped off his face and stood up. "Now listen up, troops. The Russian ambassador is a very important guest. With your mother away, I need you to be on your best behavior. That's why I've brought in our new governess, Mrs. Gruffit."

"Duffit," she said.

"Mrs. Muffit, meet three of my children—Kermit, Ethel, and Archie."

She nodded briskly. "It's a pleasure to meet you all."

"You talk funny!" I said.

Ethel elbowed me. "Archie!"

"Mrs. Ruffit is from England," explained my father.

No wonder I didn't understand her. She spoke English.

"Now, children," my father said, "I want you all to mind Mrs. Buffit just as you mind your mother and me."

Kermit said, "When have we ever misbehaved?"

"Let's see," said my father. "How about the day you slid down the grand staircase on silver trays? Or when you roller-skated on the East Room floor before the varnish had dried? Or the time a certain daughter pulled a garter snake from her dress? Or Archie threw spitballs on Andrew Jackson's portrait?"

That last part wasn't true. I didn't throw the

spitballs. I placed them. It made Andrew Jackson look like he had earrings.

"And no bringing the pony inside," said my father. "A three-hundred-fifty-pound animal doesn't belong in the White House elevator." He turned to James. "By the way, did housekeeping clean that up?"

"Yes, sir. But I'll double-check."

"That'd be bully. We wouldn't want the Russian ambassador to step in a pile of you-know-what."

Chuckling, my father nodded to James, who picked up Mrs. Duffit's bag. "I'll show you to your room," said James, and the two of them left.

Ethel looked at Kermit. "I told you it was a bad idea to bring that pony inside."

"It would have worked if the horse hadn't made so much noise," Kermit replied.

"Would not have worked," said Ethel.

"Would too."

"Would not."

"Would too."

"Would not."

"Children," said my father.

"Timid!" accused Ethel.

"Bookworm!" said Kermit.

"Stop!" yelled my father.

He looked back and forth between Kermit and Ethel. He glanced over at me, then rolled his eyes and threw his hands in the air. Watching him, I realized just how hard his job was. Almost as hard as being president.

2.

Yo-Ho-Ho!

With James and Mrs. Duffit gone, it was just the three of us, alone in the library with my father. He gathered us around him.

"Children," he said, "tonight is a very special night. I'm counting on you to behave."

"What's so special about it?" asked Ethel.

He checked to make sure no one was listening, then said in a low voice, "Can you keep a secret?"

I love secrets. It's one of the reasons I like being at the White House. Even the rooms have secrets. There's no telling how many confidential meetings and covert negotiations have taken place within these walls.

"Don't tell anyone," said my father, "but tonight,

the Russian ambassador and I are hoping to negotiate an end to the Russo-Japanese War."

It would be easy to keep that secret. I didn't even know what the Russo-Japanese War was.

Kermit must have known. He said, "Why can't the Russians negotiate to end the war on their own?"

My father snorted. "Because their ruler is a preposterous little creature who was unable to make war, and now he's unable to make peace. Don't quote me on that."

Just then James and Mrs. Duffit came back into the room. James announced, "Mr. President, the Russian ambassador is here."

"Thank you, James," my father replied. Turning to us, he said, "Peace and quiet. Just for one night."

James studied my brother, sister, and me, as if trying to imagine us being quiet. He shook his head and sighed. "Maybe you could read a book together."

"Bully!" said my father.

You may have noticed that's one of his favorite expressions. It means he's excited. He says it a lot, because he's excited a lot.

"What are our choices?" Kermit asked him.

"Anything. If you like the Greeks, I have Aeschylus, Sophocles, and Euripides."

"Too old," said Kermit.

"What about Shakespeare? *Henry the Fourth*, *Henry the Fifth*, *Richard the Third*."

"Too violent," said Ethel.

Scratching his chin, my father said, "Poetry perhaps? There's Tennyson, Longfellow, Keats, and Poe."

"Too poetic," said Kermit.

"Well," said my father, "I suppose I could lend you the book I'm reading. It's about the War of 1812."

I said, "The War of 1812? When was that?"

For some reason they all stared at me. I wish they wouldn't do that.

Something on the bookshelf caught my father's eye. He took it down and gazed at it. "Huh, *Treasure Island*. I don't remember this being here."

"What's *Treasure Island*?" I asked him.

"A story by Robert Louis Stevenson."

"Have you read it, Father?" asked Ethel.

Nodding, he looked off into the distance. "When I was punching cattle in the Badlands. One of the best stories I've ever read, all about pirates and buried treasure and adventure on the high seas."

Pirates? Buried treasure? Adventure? I went over beside him and gazed at the book.

"Funny," said my father, "but I don't remember having a copy here."

He opened the book. There was a name written inside the cover: Jura Roams.

"James," said my father, "who's Jura Roams?"

"No idea, sir."

He handed the book to James. "Why don't you take this and ask the staff? I don't think this is mine."

"Pop, wait," I said. "Is it a book we'd like?"

"Hard to say. It might be too old, too violent, or too poetic. After all, it does have a one-legged pirate who keeps saying, 'Fifteen men on the dead man's chest, yo-ho-ho and a bottle of rum.'"

This book was sounding better all the time.

"So what's it about?" asked Ethel.

My father said, "You've read it, haven't you, James?"

"Absolutely. A young boy named Jim Hawkins discovers a map and competes with the pirate Long John Silver in search of buried treasure."

"You know," said my father, "now that I think about it, it might be too scary for Archie."

"No, it's not!" I blurted.

My father raised one eyebrow. "What do you think, James?"

"He just might be old enough for it."

"Mrs. Sluffit?" asked my father.

"Duffit," she said, eyeing me. "Yes, I think maybe a good scare is just what he needs."

What did she mean by that?

Whatever she meant, my father barely noticed. "Then it's decided. *Treasure Island* it is!" Handing the book to Kermit, he said, "Just remember—peace and quiet. Now, come on, James. We've got work to do."

When they were gone, Mrs. Duffit turned to us. "All right, children, time to read."

"Yes, Mrs. Buffit," said Kermit.

"Yes, Mrs. Gruffit," said Ethel.

"Yes, Mrs. Luffit," I chimed in.

She gazed at us, and a chill settled on the room. "You may think that's funny. But I advise you to be careful. I'm not as harmless as I look."

3.

A Treasure Map

Mrs. Duffit left to unpack her bags, and the three of us clustered around the book. Ethel thumbed through the pages. "I'll read the even chapters. Kermit, you read the odds."

"What about me?" I asked.

Kermit ruffled my hair. "You get to say, 'Fifteen men on the dead man's chest, yo-ho-ho and a bottle of rum."

I began, "Fifteen men on the dead man's—"

"But only on cue," said Kermit.

"Aw, fiddlerat," I said.

Taking the book, Ethel moved over to the sofa, and

we crowded in beside her. Opening it, she began to read. "'Chapter One. Squire Trelawney, Dr. Livesey, and the rest of these gentlemen having asked me to write down the whole particulars about Treasure Island, from the beginning to the end, keeping nothing back but the bearings of the island, and that only because there is still treasure—'"

As she turned the page, a torn piece of paper fell from the book and fluttered to the floor. Ethel picked it up and examined it.

"What's that?" I asked.

Ethel said, "It looks like part of an old blueprint or something."

Looking over her shoulder, we saw a building plan, the kind that architects draw. Kermit said, "Looks like a section of the White House." Pointing to the plan, he said, "There's the library, the room we're in right now. There's the old Cabinet Room, next door. What's on the other side of the paper?"

Ethel turned it over. "There are some poems," she said. "Listen to this:

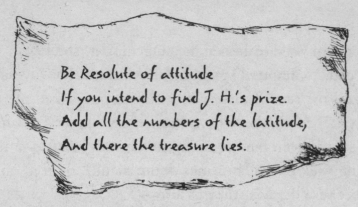

Be Resolute of attitude
If you intend to find J. H.'s prize.
Add all the numbers of the latitude,
And there the treasure lies.

"And the poem is signed 'Jura Roams.'"

"Hey," I said, "that's the same person whose name is inside the book!"

Kermit said, "There are other poems, too. Here's one:

Now in red, yet spared of flames,
This father the next clue gives.
Look up above the Constitution
To see where the treasure lives.

"This one is also signed 'Jura Roams.'"

Who was Jura Roams? Why did he write the poems? Was he still alive? It was a mystery. And I love mysteries almost as much as I love secrets.

Kermit said, "What do these riddles have to do with *Treasure Island*?"

"All the riddles say something about treasure," said Ethel. "So maybe this isn't just a random piece of paper. Maybe it's a treasure map!"

She turned the paper back over, and we studied the building plan. Was it really a treasure map? Then I realized that something was missing.

"How can it be a treasure map when there's no 'X marks the spot'?" I asked. "Treasure maps always have that."

"The edges are torn," said Kermit. "Maybe this is only part of the map."

Ethel's eyes shone with excitement. "What if the poems aren't just riddles, but clues? Maybe Jura Roams, or whoever, wanted to leave a record of hidden treasure, but one that can only be found by people smart enough to solve the riddles."

"Like us!" I said.

Kermit shot me a look. I don't know why. I'm good at riddles! I decided to demonstrate.

I said, "'Brothers and sisters have I none, but this

man's father is my father's son.' Well, who is it?"

"Archie—"

"It's me. Get it? *I'm* my father's son. Because if I don't have any brothers and sisters, then 'this man's father' is Pop, and 'my father's son' is me. So there."

"Did you fall on your head again?" asked Kermit.

"No," I said. "Not today."

I don't know what that had to do with it.

Kermit turned back to Ethel. "You're saying there might be buried treasure on White House property? Like . . . valuables from George Washington?"

"Exactly," said Ethel. "Or from Thomas Jefferson."

"Or Millard Fillmore?" I asked.

Ethel nodded. "Anyone famous in history. Like Lewis and Clark. Or Frederick Douglass."

"Or Paul Bunyan?" I asked.

"This is great!" said Kermit. "America's greatest treasures, just waiting for us to find them."

I gazed around the room. Was Jura Roams out there someplace? He could be close by. Maybe he was a spirit, floating around, watching us, drifting from room to room.

Ethel set the book on the floor, then looked back

at the paper and read, "'Be Resolute of attitude if you intend to find J. H.'s prize.' So who's J. H. and what's his prize?"

Kermit said, "I want to know who Jura Roams is. He wrote the note."

We didn't say anything for a minute. We were thinking. It's hard work. You should try it sometime.

We were still thinking when James came back. He crossed the room to my father's desk, opened a drawer, and began looking through it. Then he glanced up. "It's awfully quiet in here."

I caught Kermit's eye. "It's because we're reading," he said.

"With the book on the floor?"

Kermit shifted nervously. "Oh, that. Yes. Well. You see, we were just taking a break and having a discussion about what we read."

"You're already having a discussion about the book?" asked James. "Without having finished it?"

"Oh yes," said Ethel. "We find it's far more beneficial to discuss it as we go along."

"I see. And what discoveries have you made so far?"

Kermit said, "Personally, I'm impressed with the author's ability to transform the hero into someone so empathetic, vis-à-vis the antagonist who, in contrast, represents man's inhumanity to man and the inability of a society to nurture itself."

I whispered to Kermit, "What did you just say?"

He whispered back, "I have absolutely no idea."

James pulled out a folder, glanced through it, then closed the desk drawer. "You sure you're not up to something?"

We smiled like little angels. How could anyone doubt us?

James took one last look, then left the room. As soon as he was gone, we turned back to the treasure map.

"Now," said Ethel, "what was the rest of that first clue?"

Kermit read, "'Add all the numbers of the latitude, and there the treasure lies.'"

"What's a latitude?" I asked.

"It's an imaginary line on the planet that runs parallel to the equator," said Kermit. "It lets you know your position at all times."

I grinned at Ethel. "I thought that was an older sister's job."

Ignoring me, she pointed to the paper. "Look at that riddle. What do you see?"

"The penmanship is terrible," said Kermit. "The *t*'s are barely crossed. The letters aren't connected. I mean, even Archie has better handwriting."

Okay, maybe my handwriting isn't so great. But did they have to talk about me like I wasn't even there?

I said, "I can hear you, you know. I'm right here." I planted myself directly in front of Ethel and waved my arms.

She looked right past me.

"I don't mean the handwriting," Ethel told Kermit. "I mean the spelling. Look at the word *Resolute*. Don't you think it's odd that it's capitalized even though it's not the beginning of a line?"

Kermit shrugged. "Maybe whoever wrote it was just a bad speller."

"Or," said Ethel, "maybe it's the name of someone."

"Or some*thing*," said Kermit. He stood up and

began pacing back and forth excitedly. "What do you know about Pop's desk? You know, the one in his study."

I thought of the big wooden desk. All I knew was that it was a good place to hide.

Ethel said, "I think it used to belong to another president. So?"

"So," said Kermit, "the desk was made from timbers that were salvaged from the ruins of a British ship. The ship was found half a century ago, abandoned in the Arctic Ocean, by an American whaling ship. They rescued it, fixed it, and gave it back to England."

"Nice of them," said Ethel.

Kermit continued, "Years later, when the ship was ready to be scrapped, the English took it apart and made a desk out of it. They gave it to President Hayes, and ever since, all the presidents have used it."

"How do you know this stuff?" I asked.

"Pop told me."

Ethel said, "That's interesting, but what's it got to do with the riddle?"

Kermit beamed. "The name of the British ship was the HMS *Resolute*."

As he said the words, the wind blew. The house groaned, and the windows rattled like the bones of a skeleton.

I said, "Anyone else hear that?"

Ignoring me, Ethel looked up at Kermit. "Are you sure about this?"

"Positive."

Ethel jumped to her feet. "So all we need to do is go to the desk, and that should lead us to the treasure."

Kermit's grin faded. "We can't go into Pop's private office. We might get in trouble."

"Come on, Kermit, don't be so timid," said Ethel. Rising to her full height, she pointed forward, the way my father must have done when he led the Rough Riders up San Juan Hill. "The desk!"

I fell in next to her. "The desk!"

Kermit looked back and forth between us, then sighed. "The desk."

Ethel extended her hand. Kermit put his hand on hers, and I slapped mine on top.

"One for all!" she said.

"All for one!" he said.

I grinned. "Fifteen men on the dead man's chest, yo-ho-ho and a bottle of rum!"

4.

The Resolute

Pop's study is in one of the newest parts of the White House, where there are long, winding hallways. It's easy to get lost, especially if the lights are out. The study is a room full of books. Over it all hangs a portrait of Abraham Lincoln. My father says he likes working there, because if he has any questions, he can ask Abe.

The office was empty that night when we peeked through the doorway.

"Aaargh, mateys!" I said in my best pirate voice. "The coast is clear."

I slipped inside, and the others followed.

"Archie, you're not a pirate," said Kermit.

"I practically am."

Ethel said, "Come on now, boys, we've got things to do."

"How can you practically be a pirate?" Kermit asked me.

I opened my mouth to show him. "All I'm missing is a gold tooth!"

"Boys!" Ethel exclaimed.

We wheeled around.

"Shhhhh!" Ethel faced us, hands on her hips. "I just want to remind you, we didn't come to argue. We came for the *Resolute*."

She gestured toward a big wooden desk. Dark with age, it had detailed patterns carved into it. Maps were mounted over it, and books and papers were stacked on top.

Kermit took a deep breath. "Well, here's one way to find out what the clue is."

He got on his hands and knees and began crawling around and under the desk. Ethel and I joined him, bumping heads and bruising shins.

"Ow!" I said, rubbing my forehead. "What exactly are we looking for?"

Kermit said, "Anything that has to do with lati-tude."

"And you're positive this desk is from the *Resolute*?" Ethel asked him.

"Absolutely. I heard Pop telling one of the servants that the ship was abandoned—"

"In latitude seventy-four degrees forty-one minutes north, longitude one hundred one degrees twenty-two minutes west on fifteen May 1854," I said.

Kermit stared at me. "Hey, I'm the one who's sup-posed to finish sentences."

"Archie, how did you know that?" asked Ethel.

"What, I'm not allowed to know things?"

Ethel and Kermit looked at each other, then said in unison, "No."

I shrugged. "Okay, I read it off this plaque."

I pointed to a brass plate fastened underneath the desk. They crowded in beside me to see it.

Ethel read, "'The ship was purchased, fitted out, and sent to England as a gift to Her Majesty Queen Victoria by the President and People of the United States, as a token of goodwill and friendship.'"

Kermit continued, "'This table was made from her timbers when she was broken up, and is presented by the Queen of Great Britain to the President of the United States.'"

"Wow," I said.

"So this really is the *Resolute*," said Ethel. "Now what?"

Suddenly an explosion rocked the room. We scrambled out from under the desk just in time to see my father stride into the office. The explosion had been the sound of him slamming the door.

"What are you scoundrels up to?" he demanded.

"Up to?" said Kermit meekly.

"Yes! What are you doing in this room?"

Kermit said, "Reading."

Ethel said, "Playing."

I said, "Thinking."

Raising one eyebrow, my father gave us a funny look. We glanced back and forth at one another, trying to think of something else to say.

Kermit held up *Treasure Island*. "Just reading how . . ."

"To play . . . ," said Ethel.

"At thinking," I added.

"In my office?" asked my father.

Kermit said, "We thought it was more conducive to the spirit of the book if we read it here."

"Under my desk?"

Thinking fast, I answered, "Sure, because, see, your desk is a former ship, and much of *Treasure Island* takes place on a ship, so it just seemed like a natural fit. Ship, *Treasure Island*. *Treasure Island*, ship. You can almost hear the waves crashing and the ship creaking."

"I see," said my father. "And this helps you visualize the book?"

Kermit said, "Oh yes."

Ethel said, "Immensely."

I said, "I can practically taste the salt air."

Ethel said, "Father, have you finished negotiations?"

"No, I just have to change jackets. The Russian ambassador was making a point, and at the time he was eating a spoonful of borscht."

Just then James entered, carrying a clean jacket. "Here you are, Mr. President."

"Of course," said my father, "if he wasn't so near-sighted he might have noticed that I was standing right in front of him."

As James helped him change jackets, Mrs. Duffit entered, worried and out of breath.

"Oh, there you are, children."

My father said, "Mrs. Cuffit?"

Mrs. Duffit started to correct him, then shook her head and sighed. "Yes, Mr. President."

"You might want to keep an eye on these rapscallions tonight. I have a feeling they're up to something."

She eyed us suspiciously. "I have the same feeling, Mr. President."

He straightened up, brushed off the new jacket, and turned to James. "I'd better get back in there. Those Russians don't like to be kept waiting."

The two of them left, and Mrs. Duffit took charge. "I need to get my needlepoint from the other room. When I come back, I expect to see you three reading again."

She started for the door, then turned back. A cold breeze blew.

You know," she said, "I don't like it when children run away from me."

"W-we're sorry," I said.

"Yes," she said thoughtfully. "I think you will be."

5

The White House in Flames

As soon as the door closed, Kermit turned to Ethel and me. "Come on, we don't have much time. We've solved the first part of the riddle. What's the second part again?"

Ethel pulled out the piece of paper and read, "'Add all the numbers of the latitude, and there the treasure lies.'"

I didn't get it. What did latitude have to do with the treasure?

Kermit knelt beside the plaque. "According to this, the latitude is seventy-four degrees forty-one minutes."

"Which means that we add seventy-four and forty-one," said Ethel.

Kermit nodded. "Which equals one hundred fifteen."

I still didn't know what it meant. "So what do you think? Is it one hundred fifteen yards from the front door?"

"Or maybe one hundred fifteen paces from this very spot," said Kermit. He scrambled to his feet and looked around the room.

Ethel said, "I hate to burst your bubble, Sherlocks, but it says to add *all* the numbers of the latitude."

All the numbers? What was she talking about?

Ethel must have seen the puzzled expression on my face, because she explained, "We came up with one hundred fifteen. But now we need to add each of those separate digits—the one plus the one plus the five. Which gives us seven."

Kermit faced her, hands on his hips. "How do we know that's the right way to add the numbers? Instead of adding seventy-four and forty-one, maybe we're supposed to break it down even further. You know, add seven plus four plus four plus one."

"That doesn't make sense," Ethel told him.

"It makes just as much sense as your way."

"Fine," she said. "So seven plus four plus four plus one . . ."

"Equals sixteen," said Kermit, adding the numbers quickly. I added them in my head, trying to keep up with him.

Ethel said, "And if we break down sixteen, we add one plus six to get . . ."

They stared at each other. I stared too, because I had just gotten the same answer they did.

"Seven," we said in unison.

"Just like before," said Ethel.

As she spoke, there was another gust of wind. The house shook and groaned.

"Am I the only one hearing that?" I asked.

Ethel crossed her arms. "All right, then, are we agreed on the number seven?"

When Ethel crossed her arms, it was best to agree. Kermit and I had learned that the hard way.

"Yes," we said together.

"So," she went on, "seven is the first clue. But seven what?"

"Seven seas," I said.

"Seven wonders of the world," Kermit said.

"Seven deadly sins," Ethel said.

I had another idea. "Don't forget the seven continents."

"Archie," said Ethel, "there are only six continents."

"No, there are seven: Asia, Africa, North America, South America, Europe, Australia, and uh . . . Puerto Rico!"

"The number could be referring to time," said Kermit. "Maybe the treasure will appear at seven o'clock."

Ethel scratched her chin. "Well, then," she said, "there's only one thing left to do."

I had no idea what she was talking about, so I said the first thing that popped into my head. "Dress up like pirates and make the Russian ambassador walk the plank?"

"I was thinking more of solving the next riddle," said Ethel.

"So read it," said Kermit.

Ethel looked back down at the paper. "Here it is:

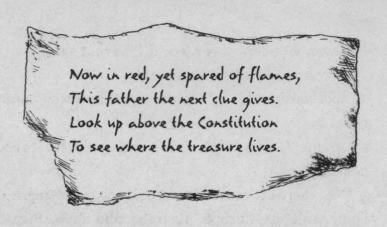

Now in red, yet spared of flames,
This father the next clue gives.
Look up above the Constitution
To see where the treasure lives.

"What do you think?"

Kermit and I looked over her shoulder. He said, "Could it mean the Constitution of the United States?"

"I guess," said Ethel. "But what's that about 'Now in red, yet spared of flames'?"

As we gazed across the room, thinking, James came in. Ethel quickly hid the paper behind her back.

Kermit's eyebrows did a funny little dance, the way they do when he's nervous. "Hello, James," he said. "What brings you back?"

James crossed the room, glancing at Ethel as he went. "Your father needs a book from his desk. So what's that piece of paper?"

"Wh-what piece of paper?" said Ethel.

"The one in your hand."

Ethel and Kermit tried to act surprised. She said, "Oh, this piece of paper! Kermit, he means this piece of paper."

"That piece of paper? The one in your hand?"

"Yes," said Ethel. "Which is funny, because I didn't even know it was there."

"I didn't either," said Kermit, "not until James pointed it out."

Ethel said, "I looked down, and, poof—there was a piece of paper."

"Right in your hand," said Kermit.

"Right in my hand," said Ethel.

James looked back and forth between them. "So," he said, "what is it?"

Why were they pretending? I decided to tell James. "It's a treasure map!"

Ethel and Kermit glared at me.

"Well, it is," I said.

"Is that true?" asked James.

I shrugged. "It's not really a treasure *map*. It's more like a treasure *riddle*."

James walked over, and Ethel showed him the

paper. He asked her, "Where did you find it?"

"It dropped out of *Treasure Island*."

Suddenly James's face went blank, and he turned away. There was something strange about the way he did it.

"Wait a minute," said Ethel, "you know something."

"Why do you say that?" asked James.

Kermit said, "Because of that look on your face. You're acting like we did when we snuck the pony upstairs."

Of course, with the pony it had been harder to pretend that nothing was wrong. How do you ignore a horse on an elevator, especially when it has an accident on the way up?

"That sure was fun," I said. "Boy, what a smell!"

"The point is," said Ethel, "I think he's heard of the treasure. Haven't you, James?"

James said, "You can't work here as long as I have and not hear about buried treasure."

"Really?" I said. We gathered eagerly around him.

"So where is it?" asked Kermit.

"And what is it?" asked Ethel.

"No one knows for sure," said James. "But there's been talk of it for years."

"How come no one's found it?" I asked.

"Maybe because no one's found a map," said James. "You three are the first. May I see it?"

Ethel handed him the paper, and he studied it for a moment. "So," said James, "one side is part of a map, and the other side has riddles."

"We solved the first riddle," I said proudly. "It took us to Pop's desk. But we're stuck on the next one."

As James read the second riddle, Ethel watched him carefully. "You know what it means, don't you?"

"I have an idea," said James. "You've heard that the White House was nearly burned to the ground?"

Ethel studied the paper. "You think that's what 'spared of flames' is referring to? The White House?"

James went to the shelves and picked out a book. Opening it on the desk, he showed us pictures as he talked. "During the War of 1812, the British were just outside Washington. James Madison was president then, and he had gone off to watch that day's battle."

As we looked at the pictures, I could almost hear

the thunder of the cannons and smell the smoke.

James went on, "President Madison advised his wife, Dolley Madison, to leave the White House. But she said that as the president's wife, she had a responsibility to stay right here."

"Even though the British were just outside of town?" asked Kermit.

James nodded. "All day she heard cannons coming closer and closer, and the sounds of horses' hooves on the streets as more and more people fled Washington. It was pandemonium. Soon the British entered Washington. They came marching up Pennsylvania Avenue, torching one building after another."

"Why?" I asked.

"The British thought that by burning the public buildings in America's capital, it would hurt the people's spirit. There was one building they especially wanted to burn."

"The White House!" I said.

"What about Dolley Madison?" Ethel asked him. "What did she do?"

"The only thing she could—escape. But first, she

tried to save as many things as possible."

"Like what?" I asked.

"Silver. Antique vases. But the most precious thing to her was also the most difficult to save: Gilbert Stuart's portrait of George Washington. It was the first piece of art ever acquired by the White House. Dolley Madison refused to leave without it."

"What made it so difficult to save?" asked Kermit. "How hard can it be to take a picture down?"

James said, "It was screwed to the wall, and they couldn't get it free. They heard the army getting closer and closer, and the servants begged the First Lady to go, but she refused. She wouldn't leave without that portrait. So they did the only thing they could think of."

"What?" I asked. "What did they do?"

"They smashed the frame," said James. "Then they pulled out the canvas painting and ran for the wagons, escaping just in time. When the enemy troops arrived, they set fire to the White House. All that was left standing were the exterior sandstone walls, smeared black from the flames."

James closed the book and put it back on the shelf.

The sound of the cannons faded, and the smoke cleared.

"So," said Kermit, "the portrait of George Washington is what was 'spared of flames'?"

"That would be my guess," said James.

I remembered seeing the painting somewhere. "It's a big one, isn't it?" I asked.

"That's right."

"But why does the riddle say 'now in red'?" asked Kermit.

James grinned. "Where's the painting?"

"Oh, I see," said Kermit. "The Red Room!"

The three of us took off for the door. As we were leaving, Ethel stuck her head back inside.

"Thanks, James!"

"How do you know so much?" I asked him.

James smiled mysteriously. "A fellow can learn a thing or two if he listens."

6.

Mrs. Duffit's Secret

I could see why they called it the Red Room. Other than white paneling around the room, it was covered in red wallpaper, which gave the place a warm glow. Portraits covered the walls, and over the fireplace was the biggest one of all: George Washington, first president of the United States. His eyes seemed to follow us as we came running into the room.

Kermit stared up at the portrait. "I've never really paid attention to it before, but it's huge."

"It's magnificent," Ethel said.

"It's hunificent," I said.

Well, it was.

Kermit pushed a chair under the painting and

stepped up to take a closer look. I noticed he wasn't acting timid anymore. Ethel must have wanted to test him, because she said, "Father doesn't like us climbing on the furniture. Aren't you afraid you'll get in trouble?"

"You know, Ethel," he answered, "sometimes you just have to grow up."

Ethel grinned. "In that case, let me up there," she said, hoisting herself up beside him.

"Me, too," I said. "Ready or not, here I come!"

I jumped up on the chair, knocking Ethel sideways. Steadying herself, she gave me one of those big-sister looks. I stuck out my tongue.

"Archie, will you stop it?" said Kermit. "We've got work to do."

He turned back to the portrait of George Washington. The three of us gazed at it in awe.

"What do you see?" asked Ethel.

"Nothing yet," said Kermit.

We looked harder. We were looking so hard that we didn't notice someone else enter the room. A booming voice said, "Found the treasure yet?"

It was my father. We scrambled down off the chair.

"T-treasure?" stuttered Kermit. "What treasure?"

"The one in your book," he said. "You know, *Treasure Island*. Has Jim Hawkins found the treasure yet?"

Oh, that treasure! I'd almost forgotten it.

"Not exactly," said Ethel. "I mean, almost, but not yet."

"So," my father said, "you're taking a break from the book to admire the Washington portrait?"

"Yes!" said Kermit. "That's it."

"We love this picture," said Ethel.

"I see," said my father.

I checked the front of his jacket. "So, Pop, where's the Russian ambassador? Did he spit on you again?"

"Archie!" said Ethel.

Just then, Mrs. Duffit came hurrying into the room, out of breath. "So, this is where you children have been hiding."

"Hello, Mrs. Fridgit," said my father.

"Duffit," she snapped.

"Mrs. Widget," he said, "is there a full moon tonight?"

"Not that I know of, Mr. President."

"Then what do you think has gotten into these three?"

She said, "I have no idea. But they're up to something."

"I think so, too," he said. "Which leads me to one conclusion. You know what they need?"

Kermit looked over at me. "Oh no."

"Here it comes," said Ethel.

"Let me guess," I said. "The strenuous life?"

Pop slapped me on the back, almost knocking me off my feet. "That's my boy!" he cried.

Clasping his hands behind his back, my father paced the room, jabbing the air with his finger, and delivered his favorite speech. He gave the speech anytime, anyplace, at the slightest excuse. I would tell you his version, but you might nod off. So I'll give you mine.

Childhood. Asthma. Weak. Puny.

Nature. Exercise. Discipline. Bootstraps.

Bronco busting. Cattle driving. Mountain climbing. Rough riding.

The hard life. The strenuous life. You can do it too!

When he got to the end of his speech, we recited the

last lines with him: "Life is a great adventure! And the worst of all fears is the fear of living!"

My father had been giving us that speech for as long as I could remember. He had been sickly as a boy and, through hard work and determination, had made himself into a hunter, a soldier, and finally president of the United States. He was worried that we had things too easy, but I didn't think it was true. For one thing, we had to listen over and over again to that speech!

"Thank you, Father," said Ethel.

Kermit nodded. I yawned. "Thanks, Pop," we said.

"Dee-lighted!" he said. "Now, the next time I see you children, I expect that book to be finished."

He started for the door, then stopped. "And no more standing on the furniture."

When he was gone, Mrs. Duffit faced the three of us. I didn't like the look in her eye.

"You may be able to fool your father," she said, "but you can't fool me. You have some secret, I can tell. Well, if you find it, then I'm going to know you've been lying to me. And believe me, there will be consequences to pay."

My father looked back into the room. "Coming, Mrs. Haffit?"

"Right away, Mr. President."

He left. She followed, then turned to us with a creepy grin on her face. "Don't forget. Con-se-quences."

When she was gone, I shivered. "I thought governesses were supposed to be nice."

Ethel said, "I thought governesses were supposed to be human."

Kermit started to climb up on the chair. "Come on, let's solve this clue before they come back."

"Wait a minute," said Ethel. "What did she just say?"

I replied, in my best Mrs. Duffit voice, "'Believe me, there will be consequences to pay.'"

"No, before that."

Kermit thought. "She'll know we've been lying to her."

"If what?" said Ethel.

"If . . . if we find it."

Ethel's eyes shone. "Find what? We never mentioned finding anything to her."

I didn't get it. "So?" I said.

"So," Kermit said, "how could she know that we're looking for something?"

I stared at Kermit. He stared at Ethel.

"Boys," she said, "I think Mrs. Duffit has a secret."

7.

The Ghost

There was a treasure hidden in the White House, and Mrs. Duffit might know about it. But how did she find out? And what did she know?

Kermit's face looked pinched and nervous again. "What do we do now?" he asked.

Ethel clenched her fists the way she does when she's determined. "We'll do the only thing we can do. We'll solve the puzzle."

That seemed to make Kermit feel better. He boosted himself back up onto the chair and studied the portrait. "What was the riddle again?"

Ethel said, "It's right here on the paper:

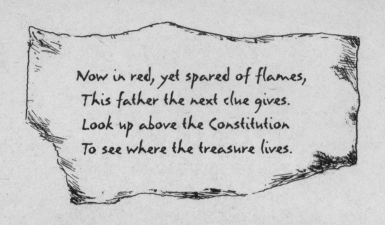

Now in red, yet spared of flames,
This father the next clue gives.
Look up above the Constitution
To see where the treasure lives.

"What do you think it means?"

Kermit searched the portrait. Ethel hopped up next to him to get a better view.

"Don't forget me," I said, crowding in beside Ethel.

Kermit said, "Look at this. In the painting, there's a book leaning against the table leg."

"You're right," said Ethel. "It says, 'The Constitution and Laws of the United States.'"

Kermit said, "That must be what the riddle means! We're supposed to look up above the Constitution."

"So what's above it?" asked Ethel.

"There's a table leg with an eagle on the corner,"

said Kermit, "a silver inkstand, a quill pen, red curtains . . ."

"There's George Washington's hand," I said.

"Keep looking," said Ethel.

Kermit said, "I don't see anything else. Unless you count the sky outside the window."

"Maybe the treasure's outside," Ethel told him.

"But where exactly? We can't just go digging up the whole yard. People would notice."

I giggled. "If they did, we could blame the Democrats."

"Why would the Democrats be digging up the White House lawn?" asked Ethel.

Kermit said, "There's got to be some way for them to get into the White House. They certainly can't get elected."

Ethel sighed. "So the answers to the first two clues seem to be 'seven' and 'outside.'"

"Whatever that tells us," said Kermit.

"Maybe the next clue will make it obvious," I said.

I hopped down from the chair to look at the clues.

Ethel and Kermit followed. Ethel sat down at the desk and spread the paper out in front of her. She said, "Here's the next one:

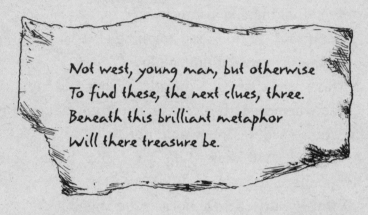

Not west, young man, but otherwise
To find these, the next clues, three.
Beneath this brilliant metaphor
Will there treasure be.

"And it's signed . . ."

"Jura Roams," said Kermit, reading over her shoulder.

"Who *is* that guy?" I asked.

"Maybe if we figure it out," said Ethel, "he could lead us to the treasure."

Kermit said, "But we've never heard of him."

Ethel looked at us with a sly grin. "We've been thinking of it as an actual name. But what if it's not? What if it's an anagram?"

"Anna who?" I said.

"Anagram," said Ethel. "It's where you're given a word or phrase that has all the letters of another word or phrase, but they're scrambled to hide the real word. You know, like *no more stars* is an anagram of *astronomers*."

"So what's an anagram of *Jura Roams*?" asked Kermit.

Closing my eyes, I leaned forward. "Our Sam Jar," I said.

"Possible," said Kermit.

I moved the letters again. "Ma As Juror."

"Perhaps," said Ethel.

"Sour Rajma," I said.

Kermit said, "We get the point, Archie."

"Rum Soraja," I added. Hey, this was fun!

"Archie!" exclaimed Kermit.

"All right, all right," I mumbled, opening my eyes.

It didn't seem fair. Finally I'd found something I was good at, and they didn't want me to do it.

"Come on," said Ethel, "let's get back to finding the treasure. The riddle says 'the next clues, three.' So maybe we're looking for three clues in one."

I read over the riddle again. "What does it mean by

'not west, young man, but otherwise'?"

Ethel shrugged. "I don't know. Maybe another direction."

"You mean, like north or south?" I said.

Kermit glanced over at Ethel. "Or east!" they said together. Without another word, the two of them raced from the room.

I looked around. Did I just miss something?

I started to follow them out, but then I heard a strange sound. It was like the rattle of bones. Like the creak of old joints. Like feet dragging across the floor.

"Hello?" I said. "Is someone there?"

A white shape appeared across the room, with slumped shoulders and gleaming eyes. "Archie . . . ," it moaned.

It looked like a ghost. It sounded like a ghost. But my parents had taught me there was no such thing. So I spoke up in a shaky voice.

"Wh-who's there?"

"Archie . . ."

I wanted to run from the room, but my father always said to be brave. "Can I help you?"

Its voice was dry as parchment. "Solve the puzzle, Archie, before the others do."

"Wh-what others? You mean Mrs. Duffit?"

The voice said, "Find the treasure before the others."

Okay, I was scared, but I was also starting to get upset. I don't like taking instructions from my parents, let alone from a figment of my imagination.

"But I'm just a kid," I said. "I don't know that I can really—"

"Find the treasure," repeated the voice. "Before the night is out, Archie, find the treasure. Find the treasure. Find the treasure . . ."

The voice faded out. The shape melted away. I stood there alone in the room. Did I mention that I don't like being alone?

"Um, okay," I said. "Can I go?"

The wind howled. An open door beat against the side of the house. Or maybe it was the sound of my heart.

I said, "Okay, I'm leaving now."

I began to walk backward, slowly and carefully. I felt my way across the room. When I reached the door, I went screaming into the night.

8.

Another Mystery

KermitEthelKermitEthelKermitEthel!" I yelled. I tore off down the hallway. I didn't know where I was going, but I knew who I was looking for. Finally, at the end of the hall, I saw two familiar figures crouched by a door.

"KermitEthelKermitEthel!"

"Shhh!" they hissed.

"You're not going to believe what I just saw."

Kermit whispered, "Would you keep it down?"

I gasped for breath, trying to control my voice. "As soon as you left, a ghost appeared!"

Kermit glanced at Ethel and rolled his eyes.

"I'm not kidding," I said. "And it commanded me to find the treasure."

"Whatever you say," replied Kermit.

They didn't believe me. They never believed me. I was just their dopey little brother. I decided the only way they would ever listen to me was if I figured out the clues. And that's exactly what I intended to do.

"Well," said Ethel, "while you were talking to ghosts, we found another mystery."

"That's right," said Kermit. "We came here to the East Room, like the clue said. When we looked inside, the room was dark, but we saw a woman sneaking around. She climbed up on a chair and was searching for something in the chandelier."

"Did she find it?" I asked him.

"We don't know. That's when you came along."

Ethel peered into the room. "Kermit, she's gone!"

"Who is she?" I asked.

But they weren't listening. They threw open the door and raced inside the darkened room. I looked around nervously, checking for ghosts, and followed them in.

The East Room was a giant ballroom with wooden floors, marble fireplaces, and three huge chande-liers hanging from the ceiling. At the moment, the chandeliers were turned off. The only light came from the moon shining through the window.

I found Ethel and Kermit in the middle of the room, standing next to the chair that the woman had placed under a chandelier. The chair was empty. But the woman wasn't gone. Her body was slumped on the floor beside the chair, not moving. It was Mrs. Duffit.

"Is she dead?" asked Ethel.

"How should I know?" said Kermit. "I'm not a doctor."

Ethel said, "See if she has a pulse."

Kermit shuddered. "You mean touch her?"

"Okay, then," said Ethel, "find out if she's breathing. Put your ear next to her mouth."

"I'm not doing that. She might bite me."

I said, "How can she bite you if she's dead?"

"Maybe she's just pretending to be dead," said Kermit.

Ethel put her hands on her hips. "She's a governess, not a possum."

We watched as Kermit leaned down over the body, being careful not to touch it, and put his ear next to her mouth. I got ready to run.

"Well?" said Ethel.

"She's breathing," said Kermit. "But she could really stand to brush her teeth. Yuck."

Just then, we heard footsteps in the hall. I could make out my father's voice. "I think it was in the East Room," he was saying. "Let's check in there."

Kermit looked at us, panicked. "We can't let him see Mrs. Duffit lying here like this. He'll send us to our rooms, and we'll never find the treasure."

"It could be worse," I said. "He might start talking about the strenuous life."

"I have an idea," said Ethel.

Getting to her knees, Ethel crouched behind Mrs. Duffit and propped her up like a ventriloquist's dummy. As she did, my father entered the darkened room, followed by a big, burly man who wore a tuxedo. The man stepped into the moonlight for a moment. I saw that he had slick, greasy hair, a handlebar mustache, and so many medals pinned to his coat that I was surprised he could stand up straight.

Squinting, my father looked around the room. "I heard a noise. It sounded like something fell. Is everyone all right?"

"Fine," Kermit said.

"Dandy," I said.

"Peachy," Mrs. Duffit said.

Her voice sounded funny and exaggerated, which wasn't too surprising, since it wasn't her voice at all. It was Ethel, hiding in the shadows behind her. To help convince them, Ethel lifted one of Mrs. Duffit's hands and waved it, as if the governess were a puppet.

"I see," said my father. "And what are you doing?"

"Sitting," Kermit said.

"Reading," I said.

"Reading," Kermit said.

"Sitting," I said. I shrugged. "Oh, just sitting and reading."

"In the dark?" asked my father.

Kermit told him, "It's more atmospheric that way."

"And where is your sister?"

"Down the hall," Kermit said.

"Upstairs," I said.

"Upstairs," Kermit said.

"Down the hall," I said.

Kermit smiled nervously. "She's upstairs down the hall."

"I see," said my father. "Mrs. Grumpet, you're not saying much."

Ethel warbled, "It's Mrs. Duffit! And I'm only quiet because these rapscallions are running me ragged." To help convince them, Ethel used Mrs. Duffit's limp hand to pat Kermit's cheek. "The little dears," she purred.

"Mrs. Trumpet, are you catching cold?" my father asked her. "You sound a bit hoarse."

Ethel cleared her throat. "I seem to be coming down with a wee spot of fever, so you'd best not be getting too close. You know how it is when the wind blows off the Potomac on these hot summer nights. I must have caught a chill. Brrr."

With Ethel's help, Mrs. Duffit shivered and hugged herself, nearly falling over sideways as she did. Kermit propped her up, then turned back to my father, trying to change the subject.

"What brings you here, Pop?"

"The Russian ambassador asked for a tour of the White House. Allow me to introduce His Excellency Arturo Paul Nicolas, Count de Cassini."

Count Cassini, squinting through his monocle,

made a deep, elegant bow. Unfortunately, it was in the wrong direction.

"Hello," I said.

"Nice to meet you," Kermit said.

"Charmed," Mrs. Duffit said.

Count Cassini, hearing what he thought was a woman's voice, turned back around and looked in her general direction. I remembered what my father had said about the ambassador's bad eyesight.

"And who have we here?" he said in a thick Russian accent.

My father said, "That's our new governess, Mrs. Tuffit."

Count Cassini fumbled for her hand. Ethel pushed it up toward him, and he kissed it.

"Madam," he said, "is greatest pleasure to meet woman so beautiful."

From behind Mrs. Duffit, Ethel sighed. "Oh, Count Cassini."

"Mr. President," said Count Cassini, "you did not tell me you employ woman of such loveliness."

"You're right," said my father. "I didn't."

Count Cassini leaned down to Mrs. Duffit. He

thought he was whispering, but his voice was as obvious as his handlebar mustache. "Perhaps when meetings are finished with president of United States, I may have the honor of dancing with you in Russian Tea Room."

"Oh, Count Cassini," cooed Ethel, "you say the most outrageous things." Using Mrs. Duffit's hand, she reached out and slapped him playfully.

Count Cassini grinned. "Ooh, I like the woman tiger."

"Grrr," said Ethel.

"Yes, well," interrupted my father, "we do have the end of a war to negotiate. We should probably get back to it."

Count Cassini gazed wistfully at Mrs. Duffit. "Farewell, my potato blossom, but is not good-bye."

He gave her a little wave, then turned to go, bumping into the chair and then following my father out the door.

When they were gone, Ethel dropped Mrs. Duffit, who fell to the floor with a thud.

I looked at over at Ethel. "'Grrr'?"

"I think I may be sick," said Kermit.

"What about me?" said Ethel. "I was that close to drinking from a samovar for the rest of my life." She turned to me and explained, "A samovar is a Russian urn."

"What's a Russian urn?" I asked.

"About five rubles a day," said Kermit.

Ethel rolled her eyes.

"Joke," said Kermit.

"Hey, what about the treasure?" I said. "We're wasting time."

"Archie's right," said Ethel. Reaching into her pocket, she pulled out the paper, held it in the moonlight, and read, "'Beneath this brilliant metaphor will there treasure be.'"

"What's a metaphor?" I asked.

Ethel said, "It's a word that compares one thing to another, to show how they might be alike."

"Well," I said, "if the metaphor is brilliant, maybe it's the chandelier."

They stared at me. I don't know why. If you ask me, the clue had seemed pretty obvious.

"You know," said Kermit, "I think Archie is right." He turned to Ethel. "I can't believe I just said that."

Ethel gazed at the paper. "If the chandelier is the brilliant metaphor, then the treasure should be . . ."

"Right beneath it," said Kermit.

We looked at the chair, then at Mrs. Duffit, who was still slumped on the floor.

"But there's nothing here," said Ethel.

"Not now there isn't," I said. "But maybe there was something there and Mrs. Duffit beat us to it. That's what the ghost said."

"Not the ghost again," groaned Kermit.

Ethel brightened. "I just thought of something. Remember when Father said he could lend us the book he was reading?"

"Yeah," I said. "It was about the War of 1812."

Kermit said, "Hey, you think there's a connection?"

Ethel said, "Don't you think it's interesting that we're talking about a treasure that might be related to the burning of the White House, and he's reading a book on that very subject?"

"But he's always reading," said Kermit. "He goes through three books a day."

"I think it's worth checking out," said Ethel.

"Look, you two can do what you want, but I'm going upstairs."

Before we could say anything, she hurried out the door, leaving us alone in the darkness. Well, almost alone. After all, Mrs. Duffit was there too. We looked down at her. There was something creepy about the way she just lay there. For just a moment, it almost looked like she smiled.

"D-did you see that?" I asked nervously.

Kermit nodded. "I wonder if Ethel needs some help."

"Ethel!" I yelled, and we went racing after her.

9.

Shadows on the Wall

We chased Ethel down the hall, up the stairs, and into my parents' bedroom. It wasn't like a normal bedroom; after all, this was the White House. It had a desk, some chairs, and a sitting area. And the bed? It was as big as some ships. It had a fancy headboard and footboard, both of which were covered with ornate carvings. The moonlight shone through the window and glistened off the polished wood.

Ethel glanced around the room, looking for my father's book.

"You know," said Kermit, "just because he's reading about the War of 1812 doesn't mean anything."

Ethel shrugged. "Let's just see, okay?"

She spotted the book on the nightstand. Hurrying over, she picked it up and opened it to the bookmark. She read, "'If not for Dolley Madison's quick thinking, who knows what treasures would have been lost that night? And who knows what treasures remain hidden to this day?'"

It was just what we had been talking about! But how would my father have known? Why would he have been reading about it?

"Do you think Pop's looking for the treasure too?" I asked.

"He must be," said Kermit.

Ethel closed the book. "First Mrs. Duffit, now Father. I hope we're done with surprises for tonight."

Suddenly the room went black. Somebody screamed. It might have been me.

"Kermit," said Ethel in a shaky voice, "if you switched off the lights as some kind of joke, it's not very funny."

"I d-didn't do anything. I'm right next to you."

"Archie?" said Ethel.

"Hey," I said, "after seeing that ghost, I won't be turning off any lights for the rest of my life."

A flickering light appeared, throwing a shadow on the wall.

"What's that?" whispered Kermit.

"The ghost," I said. "I told you."

Kermit said in a small voice, "Maybe if we sit really, really still, it won't see us."

Ethel snorted. "Right, because ghosts can't see in the dark."

The shadow grew larger. A figure appeared in the doorway. I grabbed Kermit's arm and squeezed. He didn't seem to mind. In fact, he laughed.

"There's your ghost," he said. "It's James!"

James stood in the doorway, holding two lanterns.

"The electricity went out," he said. "Strange—that hasn't happened in months."

I said, "Can someone hit me in the chest? I think I stopped breathing."

Kermit slugged me in the chest.

"Ow!" I said. "Hey, I didn't really mean it."

James eyed us by the light of the lanterns. "And what, might I ask, are you three doing in this room?"

We glanced at each other. Kermit said, "Well, uh . . ."

James shot us a sly grin. "Are you still looking for the treasure? Because if you are, I can think of one place that hasn't been checked."

"What is it?" I asked eagerly.

James leaned forward and whispered, "The walls."

Why should we check the walls? And why was James whispering?

"What makes you say that?" asked Ethel.

"Shh!" said James. "You can never tell who's listening."

He looked around, then said in a low voice, "There's a legend that Abraham Lincoln hid a treasure in the walls."

"Lincoln?" said Kermit. "What does he have to do with all this?"

James set the lanterns on the nightstand and hoisted himself onto the edge of the big bed. We climbed up beside him.

"During the Civil War," said James, "the story goes that Lincoln ordered his staff to gather anything of value. Then he hid all those valuables without telling anyone the location."

Ethel said, "But he must have gone back for them when the war was over, right?"

"He was assassinated," said James. "The treasure was never found."

"Why didn't his wife get it, or his family?" I asked.

James said, "They never knew where it was."

Ethel's eyes opened wide. "So no one ever found it?"

"That's right," said James. "And believe me, people have looked everywhere." He glanced over at me. "That's why some people think the ghost of Lincoln is in this house. They say he's still looking for his treasure."

"But why do you think it's in the walls?" asked Ethel.

James said, "According to legend, when James Hoban designed this building, he modeled it after some mansions in Ireland that had secret storage places built right into the walls. Maybe Lincoln found a crevice where he could store the valuables."

Kermit sat up straight. "Who was that architect again?"

"James Hoban."

Kermit looked at Ethel. "Whose initials are . . ."

"J. H.!" she exclaimed. "Just like in the riddle!"

The wind rattled the windows. The walls creaked too. I wondered what secrets were hidden behind them.

Over the sound of wind, I heard footsteps. From outside the door my father called, "James, could you bring us some light out here? The Russian ambassador just lost his monocle in the caviar."

Climbing off the bed, James picked up one of the lanterns from the nightstand. "I'll leave you the other lantern," he told us. "Just don't go too far. I have a funny feeling about tonight."

When he was gone, Ethel pulled out the paper again, and we crowded in around her. Back to the mystery!

Kermit said, "All right, here's the last clue we have.

Confront the ghost
And count the birds.
'Twixt one and two
The clue's interred.

"What could that mean?"

"What's *interred*?" I asked.

"Buried," said Kermit.

Ethel said, "If the ghost is Lincoln, then it only makes sense that the clue is somewhere in Lincoln's bed."

"This is Lincoln's bed?" I asked. "Our parents sleep where Lincoln slept?"

"Actually," said Kermit, "the Lincolns never slept in it. They kept it in a guest room."

We fanned out across the big bed, searching for clues—or, in this case, birds. A moment later, Ethel called out from the headboard, "Found it! Birds. Two of them."

Kermit hurried over. "The clue's supposed to be between them somewhere, but all I see is fancy woodwork."

Meanwhile, I was inspecting the footboard. "How about this bird? Does it count?"

"That's three birds!" said Kermit.

Ethel read from the paper, "''Twixt one and two . . .' If one bird is on the footboard and the other is on the headboard, then maybe the clue is *on* the bed."

We looked around for the clue. Suddenly I had an idea.

"Or *under* it!" I said.

I hopped off the bed and crawled underneath. It was dark and creepy. There was a whole herd of dust bunnies. Finally, off in a corner, I spotted something. Grabbing it, I crawled out.

"Got it!" I exclaimed.

I hurried over to the lantern, and Kermit and Ethel gathered around. In the flickering light we saw a torn piece of paper.

"It's another section of the map," said Kermit.

Ethel nodded. "The White House blueprints. And look—they're signed by J. H.!"

"James Hoban," I said.

"There's still no 'X marks the spot,'" said Kermit, "but there's one more clue:

This riddle solve
And you'll fulfill us.
Beneath the roof, above the floors,
Ursus arctos horribilis.

"And look, here's that name again: Jura Roams."

Ethel said, "What's '*ursus arctos horribilis*'?"

Kermit shrugged. "Latin for something horrible?"

"I don't get it," I said. "What could there be that's beneath the roof but above the floors?"

"Nothing," said Kermit. "Except the attic."

Gulping, I gazed at Kermit and Ethel. They gazed at me. I had a feeling we were headed to the attic.

"B-but," I stammered, "it might be . . . haunted."

Kermit took a deep breath and extended his hand. "One for all."

Ethel put her hand on his. "All for one."

I sighed. Placing my hand on top of theirs, I said, "Ghosts and treasure, here we come!"

10.

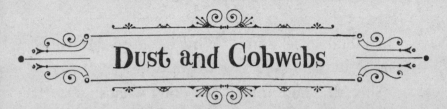

Dust and Cobwebs

I had been in the attic just once before, when I was helping James look for candlesticks before a fancy dinner. We had found them, but we had also stumbled across cobwebs, creaking floorboards, and footprints in the dust. Do ghosts leave footprints? I hadn't stuck around long enough to find out. Now, because of James Hoban and Jura Roams, I was back.

"I don't like this place," I said, pushing aside the cobwebs as I followed Kermit and Ethel into the attic. It was a long, low, dark room, with exposed beams and odd objects from a dozen presidents. To our left and right, sheets were draped over the furniture. Our shadows flickered on the walls and ceiling, thrown there by the light of Kermit's lantern.

Ethel whispered to Kermit, "Do you see anything?"

"No," he whispered back. "Do you?"

"No."

In a loud voice, I said, "Why do we need to whisper?"

"Shhhh!" said Kermit. "We don't want to disturb the ghost."

"But the clue said to confront the ghost."

"Well, yes," he replied in a shaky voice. "But only when we're good and ready."

Suddenly there was a noise.

"What was that?" asked Ethel.

I pointed off into the darkness. "I think it came from over there."

We stared across the attic, straining to see.

Ethel said, "I can't make out anything. Can you?"

Kermit and I didn't say anything. I didn't know what he was thinking, but personally, I was planning my escape.

Finally Kermit said, "I'll bet it was a mouse. Maybe it went under here."

He pulled a sheet off a large object. Underneath, with glowing eyes and sharp teeth, crouched a grizzly bear!

The three of us screamed. I was about to carry out my escape plan when I noticed something.

"Hey," I said, "it's stuffed!"

"How did that get here?" asked Ethel.

Kermit said, "You know how Pop loves to hunt. I'll bet he shot it and had it stuffed for the Oval Office."

Ethel giggled. "And Mother made him put it up here."

"Well," I said, "I don't know about you, but I wasn't scared."

"I wasn't either," said Kermit quickly.

"Neither was I," said Ethel.

We glanced around at each other, trying to look brave.

"I might need to change my trousers," I said.

Kermit grinned. "You're not a scaredy-cat, are you? A nervous Nellie? A yellow belly?"

As he spoke, a white shape appeared behind the bear. It was the ghost!

Crying out, I darted behind Kermit, who was standing motionless, frozen with fear.

"Okay," said Kermit, "now I need to change my trousers too."

Ethel was scared, but she was still Ethel. "Great. My one chance to find a treasure, and I'm paired with Tweedledum and Tweedledummer."

Kermit said, "If you're so brave, why don't you go talk to it?"

"Me?" she said. "You're supposed to be the courageous older brother."

"But it's your turn to do something," Kermit replied.

"Hey," said Ethel, "I had to impersonate Mrs. Duffit. I've done my part."

Kermit crossed his arms. "Yeah, well, I had to smell her breath. I'm scarred for life."

While they argued, I peeked out from behind Kermit and slowly inched my way forward. After all, I had met this ghost before.

I cleared my throat. "Excuse me, Mr. Ghost. Hello?"

Kermit hissed, "Archie, get back from there!"

In the same rough, halting voice I had heard before, the ghost said, "You come to speak to me again?"

"Yes, Mr. Ghost," I said, my voice quivering. "It's me again, Archie Roosevelt. This is my sister Ethel . . ."

Ethel gave a meek little wave. "Hi."

"... and my brother—"

"Malachi," blurted Kermit. "Malachi Fiferpoofing."

Ethel and I stared at him. Kermit shrugged. "I don't want some ghost knowing my real name."

The ghost drifted forward. "Find the treasure, Archie, before the others. Find the treasure."

"But we don't know where to look," I said. "We're down to our final clue, and we don't have any idea where to go next."

Pointing a bony finger, the ghost moaned, "*Ursus arctos horribilis . . . Ursus arctos horribilis . . .*"

The ghost floated backward into the darkness. A moment later it was gone.

Looking at Kermit, Ethel stifled a nervous giggle. "Well, Malachi, what now?"

"You laugh," said Kermit, "but when that ghost tracks us down, you'll realize how smart I was. Everyone will say, 'Sorry, there's no Malachi Fiferpoofing here. You must be thinking of someone else.' And poof! The ghost will try another house, and I'll be safe."

Thinking of the ghost, I considered what it had said. The words had reminded me of something.

"The next message must be in the bear!" I exclaimed

"What?" said Ethel.

"I just remembered: '*Ursus arctos horribilis*' is Latin for *grizzly bear*. Pop told us that once."

"Hey, I think you're right," said Kermit.

Ethel approached the bear. "But how would a bear send a message?"

I shrugged. "Through his pooper?"

"Archie!" said Ethel.

"Well," I told her, "that's where things come out."

She shook her head, but it made sense to me.

Kermit examined the bear. "Pop always said there was nothing scarier than when he saw grizzlies in Yellowstone Park and they let loose a growl. So maybe it's through his mouth."

Handing the lantern to Ethel, he stood on his tip-toes and peered into the bear's mouth. I figured it couldn't hurt to check the other place, so I knelt down behind the bear. I noticed a flash of white where there shouldn't have been. Taking it out, I saw that it was a piece of paper, rolled into the size and shape of one of my father's cigars.

"Hey, look what I found!" I exclaimed.

"Where did you get that?" asked Kermit.

"Just where I said to look. In his pooper!"

Ethel shuddered. Kermit said, "It doesn't matter where he found it, just that he did. Let's take a look."

He took the paper from me using the tips of his fingers. Unrolling it, he spread it on the floor, and Ethel brought the lantern closer. Kermit set the other two papers beside it, matching up their torn edges.

"They fit!" I exclaimed. "The three of them together make a perfect rectangle."

"They're the floor plans of the White House," said Ethel in wonder.

"Look," said Kermit, "the new paper has a note in the margin:

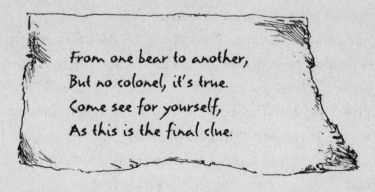

From one bear to another,
But no colonel, it's true.
Come see for yourself,
As this is the final clue.

"And there's that name again: Jura Roams."

"I don't get it," said Ethel. "'One bear to another'? 'No colonel, it's true'?"

Just then I had an idea. "Wait a minute. What was that example you gave of an anagram?"

"Archie," said Ethel, "we don't have time for games."

But I wasn't going to give up so easily. "When you were explaining anagrams, you gave an example. What was it?"

Ethel sighed. "*Astronomers*. It's an anagram for *no more stars*."

With that, everything clicked into place.

"I've got it!" I exclaimed.

"Got what?" asked Kermit.

"I know where the treasure is. Come to the roof and I'll show you!"

11.

The Treasure

I raced up the wooden steps that led to the roof. I opened the door, and suddenly I was surrounded by stars.

Two dark shapes followed me through the door. "Archie?" said Kermit in a low voice.

Ethel said, "Archie, are you there?"

"Here I am!" I said. "Do you see it?"

They approached slowly, with Kermit carrying the lantern. Its dim light illuminated the area where we stood, a flat, semicircular space above the south portico. A low wall lined the edge.

Kermit looked around. "Is there something up here you wanted to show us?"

"Not up here," I said. "Up *there*!"

"I don't get it," he said.

"Me neither," said Ethel. "And I certainly don't see any treasure."

Kermit snorted. "You just brought us up here because you were scared of that bear."

"No," I said, "I wanted to show you *this* bear."

They looked around but still didn't see anything.

"Did you fall on your head again?" asked Kermit.

I said, "You don't understand. Up there." I pointed to the sky.

"I see stars," said Kermit. "There's the Big Dipper. So what?"

"Don't you remember what Pop taught us?" I said. "The Big Dipper is part of a different constellation, a bigger one. It's called Ursa Major—Latin for *the Great Bear*. That's the treasure!"

Kermit and Ethel gazed upward in wonder. The clouds had parted, and the moon shone down on us. Next to the moon, twinkling in the darkness, was the most famous constellation in the sky.

Kermit sighed. "You mean there's no gold?"

"I think it's beautiful," said Ethel.

The wind blew. Somehow it didn't seem as frightening anymore.

"Are you sure?" asked Kermit. "What about the other clues?"

Ethel said, "I'll tell you part of it. Remember the new clue? We couldn't figure out what it meant by 'no colonel.' Now we know. It's not a colonel or a captain or a general. It's a major—Ursa Major."

"What about Jura Roams?" asked Kermit. "Who is he, and what does he have to do with Ursa Major?"

"That's simple," I said. "He *is* Ursa Major."

Kermit stared at me. "Huh?"

"Don't you see? It's an anagram. That's what I figured out in the attic. If you unscramble the letters of *Jura Roams*, you get *Ursa Major*."

Kermit's eyes lit up. "Ursa Major—Jura Roams. Of course!"

"One thing still puzzles me," said Ethel. "Remember the very first clue, when we added the numbers of latitude?"

Kermit nodded. "It was seven, right? For seven o'clock?"

"But what did time have to do with it?" she said. "That didn't help us solve anything."

I glanced up at the sky, and suddenly I knew. "It was never referring to time. It's the number of stars that make up the Big Dipper, the constellation that's part of Ursa Major."

Kermit said, "The stars are outside, so they're above and behind the Constitution, like the clue said."

"And they're sparkly, like the chandeliers," added Ethel. "That was the brilliant metaphor. *Those* lights representing *these* lights."

Something occurred to me. I turned to Ethel. "Can I see those papers again?"

She handed them to me. Kneeling, I lined them up next to each other.

"These are floor plans, right?" I said.

"Yeah," said Kermit. "So?"

"They were also a clue. Floor plans show the White House from a bird's-eye view. The treasure was never *in* the White House. It was above it all along."

We turned and gazed up at the treasure—Jura Roams, Ursa Major, glistening in the sky.

"It's gorgeous," Ethel said.

"Magical," Kermit said.

"Gormical," I said.

Ethel gathered up the papers. "How did you do it, Archie? How did you solve the mystery?"

I shrugged. "Well, as James says, a fellow can learn a thing or two if he listens. Also, there was that anagram. It got me thinking."

"Astronomers," said Kermit.

"No more stars," said Ethel.

Kermit shook his head. "I still can't believe it. Archie Roosevelt solved a mystery."

I said, "Now maybe you'll start listening to me for a change."

They looked at each other. "Nah," they said.

Just then, there was a noise from the stairway. Behind the door, steps were creaking. Someone was coming up to the roof.

"You know," said Kermit in a shaky voice, "there's one part of the mystery we never did solve."

Ethel nodded. "I was trying not to think about it."

I swallowed, then stared at the door.

"The ghost," I said.

12.

A Great Adventure

The door burst open, and a figure came hurtling through. It was my father. Following him were James and Mrs. Duffit.

"By Godfrey, what's going on?" he asked.

"Father!" said Ethel. She ran to him and gave him a big hug.

I was right behind her. "We thought you were still in negotiations."

"I was until I heard a racket up on the roof. So what are you savages doing up here?"

He had always taught us to tell the truth. Maybe it was time we did.

Ethel glanced at Kermit and me. We nodded. She faced my father. "We can explain everything. We know we were supposed to read a book . . ."

"But, well," said Kermit, "we found a treasure map, and we simply had to go looking for it . . ."

"And we added the numbers under your desk," I said, "and Washington's picture told us *where*, and the chandeliers told us *what*, and the birds on Lincoln's bed pointed to the final clue in the bear's pooper."

"Archie," said my father, "did you fall on your head again?"

"No!"

Turning to Ethel, he said, "Now, what's this about a treasure map?"

"Actually," she said, "it's a floor plan, with clues written on it." She took out the papers and showed him. He glanced at them, then tucked them into his pocket.

"And where did these clues lead you?" he asked.

"Here!" I said. "And there." I pointed to the sky.

Kermit said, "The Big Dipper. Which is part of Ursa Major."

"I see," grunted my father. Gazing upward, he recited,

> *"Now in red, yet spared of flames,*
> *This father the next clue gives.*
> *Look up above the Constitution*
> *To see where the treasure lives."*

Kermit stared at him. "How did you know that?"
Smiling, my father said,

> *"Be Resolute of attitude*
> *If you intend to find J. H.'s prize.*
> *Add all the numbers of the latitude,*
> *And there the treasure lies."*

He knew the clues! It seemed impossible. Then, slowly, it dawned on me.

"You wrote them!" I said.

My father's eyes gleamed, the way they do when he's taken a good hike or passed a new law.

Ethel said, "But how did you know we'd pick *Treasure Island* and find the map?"

Father looked at James. I could see he's been in on it too. "With a choice between Sophocles, Shakespeare, and *Treasure Island*," said James, "we were pretty sure which one you'd choose."

Thinking about the books gave me an idea.

"You know," I said to Kermit and Ethel, "now that we've found our own treasure, I want to learn about the one Jim Hawkins was looking for. Let's read *Treasure Island*—and let's finish it this time."

"That's fine," said Ethel, "but in the meantime, what do we do about him?"

"Who?" I asked.

She nodded toward the other side of the roof, where a white shape had appeared.

"The ghost!" I exclaimed, pointing. "Look, Pop!"

"Where?" he asked.

"There!"

The ghost drifted closer. With a thick Russian accent, it moaned, "Four score and seven years before . . ."

"That ghost?" said my father. "The one who sounds like a Russian?" He motioned to the ghost. "Count Cassini, would you care to join us?"

I gaped at him. "Count Cassini?"

"Children," said my father, "you remember the Russian ambassador, Count de Cassini?"

The ghost pulled off its white cloak, which turned out to be a bedsheet. "Forgive me for scaring young children. But I do what president of United States ask me to do, because I know he may softly speak, but he carry the big stick."

Kermit said, "You mean there were never any secret messages from James Hoban or Abraham Lincoln?"

"Not that I know of," said my father.

"And everyone knew but us?" I asked.

He shrugged. "I certainly couldn't have pulled it off on my own."

Ethel said, "James? The Russian ambassador? Even Mrs. Duffit?"

"Mrs. Gruffit?" said my father. "She's an actress from New York City. Her real name is Polly Mulligan. Or is it Bulligan?"

I stared at her. Suddenly I knew the answer to another mystery.

"Aha!" I said. "I bet her real name isn't even Mrs. Duffit."

"He just told us that," said Kermit.

"Oh."

My father explained, "Your mother and I used to watch her on Broadway when I was a New York City police commissioner."

The actress grinned and said in a voice that didn't sound at all like a governess, "Hey, kids. Howya doin'?"

I said, "I thought your accent sounded funny."

She waved a finger under my nose. "Watch it. Conse-quences."

"I don't get it," said Kermit. "Was any part of this true?"

"Most of it, actually," said my father.

"The story of the *Resolute*?" I asked.

"True," said my father.

"Dolley Madison saving the Washington portrait?" asked Ethel.

"True," said my father.

"Lincoln hiding valuables in the White House walls?" asked Kermit.

"That we made up," said my father. "But it's a good story, isn't it? Well done, James."

"Thank you, Mr. President."

Ethel said, "So the Russian ambassador didn't really fall for Mrs. Duffit?"

"Ah," said Count Cassini, "that part very true. It may surprise you that in Russia, women not so much this beautiful."

He looked sadly at Mrs. Duffit. He would be leaving soon, and I could tell that he didn't want to.

Kermit said, "Why did you do it, Pop?"

"You mean, why did we send you on a treasure hunt to find a constellation?"

"Yes."

My father didn't say anything. He just gazed at us.

Ethel said, "We know the answer, don't we?"

He nodded.

She said, "It's something you're always telling us, isn't it?"

He nodded.

Kermit declared, "Life is a great adventure!"

"And the worst of all fears is the fear of living!" I added

Ethel said, "By looking for the treasure—a *real* treasure—we had to overcome our fears."

"We even had to work together," I said, elbowing Kermit.

"Ow!" he said.

"But why Ursa Major?" asked Ethel. "Why was that the treasure?"

My father looked at the sky. "I figured if I was going to send you on a great chase, the end result should be pretty spectacular. And what's more spectacular than Ursa Major?"

We gazed upward in silence. Then I looked around the roof.

"All right, then," I said, "I have just one more question. If you were behind this from the beginning . . ."

"And I was," said my father.

"And James knew all about it . . ."

"That's right," said James.

"And Mrs. Duffit was a hired actress . . ."

"Hey," she said, "a woman's got to work."

"And Mr. Cassini was Lincoln's ghost . . ."

"Is true," he said.

"Then who is that?"

I pointed to a shimmering figure floating at the edge of the roof. It was white, like gauze, with stars

twinkling around and through it. As we watched, the figure nodded, then slowly faded away, leaving us staring into the night.

I looked up at my father and grinned. I didn't know who or what I'd just seen, but I was going to find out. And I knew one more thing.

It would be a great adventure.